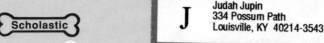

Scholastic

Clifford THE BIG RED DOG®

THE MYSTERY OF THE KIBBLE CROOK

Adapted by Liz Mills

Illustrated by Gita Lloyd and Eric Binder

**Based on the Scholastic book series
"Clifford The Big Red Dog"
by Norman Bridwell**

From the television script "Kibble Crook"
by Dev Ross

Cartwheel
·B·O·O·K·S·®

SCHOLASTIC INC.

New York   Toronto   London   Auckland   Sydney   Mexico City
New Delhi   Hong Kong   Buenos Aires

No part of this publication may be reproduced, or stored in a retrieval system, or transmitted in any form or by any means, electronic, mechanical, photocopying, recording, or otherwise, without written permission of the publisher. For information regarding permission, write to Scholastic Inc., Attention: Permissions Department, 555 Broadway, New York, NY 10012.

ISBN 0-439-33248-6

Library of Congress Cataloging-in-Publication Data available

10 9 8 7 6 5   02 03 04 05 06

Printed in the U.S.A.   23
First printing, April 2002

One day, T-Bone ran into Cleo's yard.

"Clifford! Cleo! Let's play!"

he shouted.

But no one was there.

T-Bone lay down on the grass to wait.

Then he saw Cleo's bowl.

And he smelled something good.

"I'll ask Cleo if I can try

her dog food when she gets back,"

said T-Bone.

But the longer he waited,

the better the food smelled.

T-Bone thought he would

just have a little taste.

"Wow! This food is great!"

said T-Bone.

And he took another taste.

T-Bone ate more and more…

until it was all gone!

"Oh, no!" he cried.

"I ate all of Cleo's food!

She's going to be so mad!

What am I going to tell her?"

Then Clifford, Cleo, and Mac

walked into the yard.

"I want everyone to try

my new dog food," said Cleo.

"Oh, no!" she cried.

"What's wrong?" asked Clifford.

"Somebody ate my food!" she shouted.

"Maybe a kibble crook took it,"
said Mac. "That's what you call a dog
who eats another dog's food."

Cleo turned to T-Bone.

"Did you see anyone?" she asked.

T-Bone was afraid to tell the truth.

"I think I saw a dog run down the

street," he said.

"Which way did he go?" Cleo asked.

"I think he ran toward the dock,"

T-Bone said.

"Let's go make him say he's sorry!"

said Mac.

The dogs ran off.

At the dock, the dogs sniffed right.

They sniffed left.

They looked high.

They looked low.

No kibble crook.

T-Bone stopped to scratch his ear.

"They are not going to find anything.

I'm the kibble crook," he thought sadly.

T-Bone scratched harder.

He bumped into a box next to him.

Then he heard a noise.

Bark! Bark! Bark!

It came from inside the box.

The other dogs ran over.

"That sounds like a dog to me!"
said Mac.

"Yeah," said Cleo, "and I bet it's
stuffed with my kibble!"

Clifford turned over the box with

his paw.

Lots of toy dogs were inside, barking.

"Well, Cleo, they're stuffed, but not

with your kibble!" said Clifford.

"Maybe we should give up.

It's only dog food," said T-Bone.

"That dog ate *my* kibble without

asking!" said Cleo.

"Oh, yeah," said T-Bone.

The dogs walked toward the beach.

Mac stopped in front of a cave.

"Every crook needs a hideout," he said. "This cave is perfect!"

Clifford walked up to the cave.

"Hellooooo!" he shouted.

"Hellooooo!" came an echo.

"It's the kibble crook!"

whispered Cleo.

"Let's go catch him!" said Mac.

"Wait!" T-Bone said. "I don't think you should go in there."

"Why not?" asked Clifford.

"Because I'm the one who...who..."

T-Bone stopped.

He looked at the ground.

"What?" asked Mac.

"Because I'm the one who should go in there by myself," said T-Bone.

"That's very brave of you," said Clifford. "Are you sure you don't want us to come with you?"

T-Bone nodded sadly.

He walked into the cave.

After a while, Clifford started walking back and forth. "Clifford," asked Cleo, "will you stop doing that?"

"But I'm worried about T-Bone,"

said Clifford.

Inside the cave, T-Bone thought about
how he ate Cleo's new dog food.
He thought about how he told a lie to
his friends.

And then he walked out

of the cave.

"Did you catch him, T-Bone?" asked Cleo.

"There is no kibble crook. *I* ate your new dog food, Cleo," said T-Bone. "I'm sorry."

"Why didn't you say so before?" asked Cleo.

"I was afraid you'd be mad at me," said T-Bone. "But I promise to always tell the truth from now on."

Cleo smiled. "Okay. Let's see if there's more dog food at home!"

And the dogs ran off together.

Do You Remember?

Circle the right answer.
1. Who ate Cleo's food?
   a. The seagulls
   b. Mac
   c. T-Bone

2. Near the beach, Mac found...
   a. a treasure.
   b. a cave.
   c. an anchor.

Which happened first?
Which happened next?
Which happened last?
Write a 1, 2, or 3 in the space after each sentence.

T-Bone told the truth.   _____

Cleo's food bowl was empty.   _____

The dogs searched the dock.   _____

Answers:

1. c
2. b
T-Bone told the truth. (3)
Cleo's food bowl was empty. (1)
The dogs searched the dock. (2)